Selena
the Sleepover
Fairy

Special thanks to Rachel Elliot

No part of this work may be reproduced, stored in a retrieval system,
or transmitted in any form or by any means, electronic, mechanical,
photocopying, recording, or otherwise, without written permission of
the publisher. For information regarding permission, write to
Rainbow Magic Limited, c/o HIT Entertainment,
830 South Greenville Avenue, Allen, TX 75002-3320.

ISBN 978-0-545-38476-6

All rights reserved. Published by Scholastic Inc., 557 Broadway,
New York, NY 10012, by arrangement with Rainbow Magic Limited.

SCHOLASTIC and associated logos are trademarks and/or registered
trademarks of Scholastic Inc. RAINBOW MAGIC is a trademark of
Rainbow Magic Limited. Reg. U.S. Patent & Trademark Office and other
countries. HIT and the HIT logo are trademarks of
HIT Entertainment Limited.

12 11 10 9 8 7 6 5 4 3 2 1   12 13 14 15 16 17/0

Printed in the U.S.A.   40
First Scholastic printing, May 2012

Selena the Sleepover Fairy

by Daisy Meadows

SCHOLASTIC INC.

New York   Toronto   London   Auckland

Sydney   Mexico City   New Delhi   Hong Kong

The dark cloak of midnight has
blocked out the sun,
But those silly fairies think bedtime is FUN!
They keep me awake and ruin my bad dreams
With laughter as bright as the sun's awful beams.

Sleepover Fairy, your magic I'll steal
And hide it in places I'll never reveal.
Your plans will be ruined because I'm so clever,
And sleepover fun will be banished forever!

**Find the hidden letters in the teddy bears
throughout this book. Unscramble all 8 letters
to spell a special sleepover word!**

The Magic Sleeping Bag

Contents

School Trip

"I feel like it's my birthday and Christmas all at the same time!" said Rachel Walker, bouncing up and down on her seat. "I can't believe we're actually going to a sleepover at the National Museum!"

"It makes it twice as exciting that

you're here," her best friend, Kirsty Tate, agreed, settling down beside her. "It was so nice of the principal to let you come along."

Kirsty's school had won a place in a giant charity sleepover, which was being held in the National Museum. Thirty children from the school were going to the city to participate. Rachel was staying with Kirsty for the weekend, so she had been allowed to join in, too.

The bus driver took his seat and the engine rumbled into life. As the bus pulled out of the school parking lot, the girls waved good-bye to Kirsty's mom, who had come to see them off.

"I hope it's not spooky there at night," said a girl named Hannah, who was sitting in the seat behind Rachel.

"I'm a little scared of the dark."

"Don't worry," said Kirsty with a comforting smile. "I've been there before and it's really cool. There are lots of amazing things to do."

"I want to see the Dinosaur Gallery!" said Rachel, opening a bag of candy and passing it around.

"Oh, yes. And the diamond exhibition with all the sparkling jewels," Kirsty added, taking a pink candy and popping it into her mouth.

"The marine fossils!" said Arthur.

"The wildlife garden!" said Allie.

"The world lab!" said Dan.

Suddenly there was a loud bang from beneath their feet.

"What was that?" Hannah squealed. "Did a wheel come off?"

"I don't think so," said Rachel, frowning. "It sounded like it was inside the bus."

Their teacher, Mr. Ferguson, stood up at the front of the bus.

"Don't worry, everyone," he said. "It's just our bags slipping and sliding around in the luggage area. I hope you don't have any eggs in your backpacks!"

There was a little ripple of laughter, and Hannah looked less nervous.

"Come on," Kirsty said to take Hannah's mind off her fears. "Let's play a game."

Soon Rachel, Kirsty, and their friends were playing a fun and noisy game of Go Fish. They hardly heard the occasional bangs and thumps from the luggage area and they didn't notice when the bus pulled off the highway. When it started to slow down, they looked around in surprise.

"Are we there already?" asked Kirsty.

"Not yet," said Mr. Ferguson with a smile. "We're going to stop for a break. We'll be heading out in twenty minutes, so keep an eye on your watches. Everyone must be back here by quarter after seven."

Everyone filed off the bus. Kirsty and Rachel were the last to step off. As they hurried after

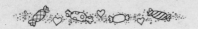

the others, Kirsty noticed that her shoelace was undone. She bent down to tie it, and Rachel waited for her.

"It's nicer here than most rest stops," she said. "I like all the greenery."

The rest stop was hidden from the highway by a line of leafy trees. As Rachel looked at them, something sparkled among the leaves. Rachel gasped.

"Kirsty, look up there!"

Kirsty stood up and clutched Rachel's hand in excitement.

"That looks like fairy dust!" she

exclaimed. "Oh, Rachel, do you think we're about to have another adventure?"

"Let's find out!" Rachel said.

The girls hurried toward the trees. They were friends with the fairies who lived in Fairyland, and often helped out when Jack Frost caused trouble. Maybe the fairies needed their help again!

Fairy Sparkles

As soon as the girls walked under the trees, the sparkles became brighter and whooshed toward them like miniature shooting stars. The blur of lights whirled around Rachel and Kirsty in hoops of purple and pink. When the blur slowed down, the girls saw a fairy hovering in front of them, her long, braided black hair gleaming in the evening sun. She was wearing a pretty white romper

trimmed in pink, and there were fluffy pink slippers on her feet. Under her arm was a little teddy bear.

"Hello," she said in a soft voice. "I'm Selena the Sleepover Fairy!"

"It's so nice to meet you," said Rachel with a smile. "We're on our way to a giant sleepover!"

"Yes, I know," said Selena, looking worried. "That's why I'm here. Your sleepover could be in trouble. Jack Frost has done something horrible!"

Kirsty gasped. "What do you mean?"

"What happened?" asked Rachel.

Selena fluttered over to a low branch

and perched on a nodding leaf.

"The Night Fairies and I organized a midsummer fairy sleepover last night," she explained. "It was so much fun! All the fairies were there, and there were games, songs, stories, and snacks."

"It sounds great," said Kirsty.

"Jack Frost didn't think so," said Selena, frowning. "He got angry because we

were having so much fun. While we were playing games in the starlight, he snuck into the meadow where we were planning to sleep."

Rachel's hand flew to her mouth. "What did he do?" she asked.

Selena bit her lip. "He stole my most precious possessions!" she said. "He knows that my three magic objects help sleepovers to go smoothly. Without them, last night was ruined. And now your big sleepover at the museum might be, too!"

"What are your magic objects?" Rachel asked.

Selena smiled as she thought about them.

"The magic sleeping bag ensures that everyone gets a good night's sleep," she said. "The enchanted game bag makes all games fun and fair, and the sleepover snack box guarantees that everyone will enjoy lots of delicious food."

"Oh, no" said Kirsty.

"Without games and food, sleepovers won't be the same!"

"Couldn't you ask Jack Frost to give them back?" Rachel suggested.

"I did," said Selena sadly. "I went to the Ice Castle and begged him to return my special things. I even told him about your charity sleepover. But he

just said that if human sleepovers were ruined, too, that would make him even happier!"

Kirsty and Rachel had been to Jack Frost's Ice Castle during other fairy adventures. It was a very scary place! Selena had been very brave to visit it all by herself. Kirsty squeezed Rachel's hand and gave Selena a reassuring smile.

"Please try not to worry," she said. "We'll help you find your magic objects. We'll do everything we can to get them back."

"Thank you!" said Selena, grinning. "The Night Fairies told me how nice you are. They suggested that I come and find you."

"The hardest part is knowing where to start looking," said Kirsty thoughtfully. "Maybe we should visit the Ice Castle ourselves and search for clues."

"I don't think we need to do that," said Rachel, sounding excited. "Look over there!"

Selena and Kirsty turned to look where Rachel was pointing, and their mouths fell open. Six goblins were climbing out of the luggage area of their bus,

carrying armfuls of backpacks and
sleeping bags!

"Those awful goblins!" exclaimed
Kirsty. "Why do they want our things?"

As the girls watched, the green
mischief-makers scampered into the rest
stop, arms piled with luggage for the
sleepover.

"People will see them!" exclaimed Rachel. She and Kirsty knew that if any other humans spotted the goblins, Fairyland could be in terrible danger. They couldn't let that happen!

Kirsty turned to Rachel, looking determined. "Come on, we have to follow them!"

A Goblin Sleepover

Kirsty, Rachel, and Selena hurried into the rest stop after the goblins. It was crowded with people, and Selena tucked herself out of sight under Kirsty's hair. On their left was a self-service cafe, where their friends were buying drinks and snacks. On their right was a gift shop, and a sign pointed to the restrooms straight ahead.

"Where did they go?" whispered Selena in Kirsty's ear.

The rest stop was so busy that it was hard to see through the crowd. Kirsty and Rachel looked all around, and then Rachel gave a cry. Among the people, she had spotted a green sleeping bag bobbing in the air. A goblin was carrying it on his head! "That way — look!"

The girls pushed their way through the crowd, dodging elbows, bags, and legs. They kept catching glimpses of the goblins ahead of them, and they could hear snatches of squabbling goblin voices.

"Get off my sleeping bag!"

"That pink backpack's mine."

"Give it back!"

The goblins were pushing and shoving one another. One of them staggered sideways into a magazine stand and knocked it over. The store manager gave an angry shout. Kirsty was so busy trying to see what was happening, she forgot to watch where she was going. Suddenly she ran into a very large man!

"Ooof!" he said in surprise, as Kirsty

stumbled backward into Rachel.

"*Ooof!*" said Rachel.

"Oh, sorry!" Kirsty exclaimed. "Are you OK?"

"No harm done," said the man with a kind smile.

But when the girls looked around again, the goblins had completely disappeared!

"Oh, no." Rachel groaned. "How are we going to find them now?"

"I have an idea," said Selena.

She gave her wand a tiny flick, and it began to glow.

"This spell will make the wand glow brighter as we get closer to the goblins," she whispered in Kirsty's ear. "Just keep walking and I'll tell you which way to go."

Guided by the glowing wand, they hurried toward the back of the rest stop until they reached an escalator. They could see only shadows beyond the escalator. Even the lights weren't working.

"There's nothing here," said Rachel, looking around. "No shops, no cafes — it's just dark and spooky."

Just then, the girls heard a giggle.
Raising a finger to her lips, Kirsty tiptoed
around the back of the escalator. The tip
of Selena's wand was glowing very

brightly! Rachel followed,
and together they poked
their heads around
the corner.
The goblins were all there,
sitting on the ground! They
had rolled out their stolen
sleeping bags and were
searching through the
backpacks for pajamas.
"Jack Frost will never
guess where we are!" One
of the goblins giggled.
He put on a pink feathered
eye mask and settled

back with a contented sigh.

"I'm not ready to go to sleep yet," said another goblin, who was wearing checked pajamas. "When do the games start?"

"Where is everyone?" asked a third goblin, looking around expectantly. "Maybe they're playing hide-and-seek."

He paced around, peering into the shadows. The girls drew back a little, confused. Why would the goblins think

there were going to be games in a rest
stop?

"It was lucky we heard that fairy
telling Jack Frost about the humans' giant
sleepover," said another goblin, pulling on
fuzzy orange socks. "I've always wanted
to go to one."

"Oh!" exclaimed Rachel with a flash of
understanding. "They must have decided
to crash our sleepover, and they think this
is it!"

"In the middle of a rest stop?" said
Kirsty. "Oh, those silly goblins!"

The goblins were already arguing.

"Shut up and go to sleep!" snapped the
eye-mask goblin.

"But I'm not sleepy," squeaked the
goblin in the checked pajamas.

"This is no fun," said a skinny goblin

who was wearing an old-fashioned
nightcap. "Sleepovers are boring!"

"*You're* boring!" snapped the goblin
with the fuzzy socks.

A teddy bear flew through the air and
hit the skinny goblin on the nose.

"OUCH!" he squawked. "You'll be
sorry you did that!"

Selena darted out from under Kirsty's hair with a cry of excitement.

"Look at his sleeping bag!" she said, pointing at the skinny goblin.

Rachel and Kirsty peered through the darkness. The sleeping bag didn't suit the goblin at all. It was pink and decorated with hearts and lollipops, and it was glowing with a soft, warm light.

"Rachel, Kirsty, that's my magic sleeping bag!" Selena told them, her eyes shining. "We found it!"

A Smelly Spell

Rachel and Kirsty gasped as they stared at the magic sleeping bag. The skinny goblin was snuggling down into it.

"We can't get it back while he's in it," Rachel whispered.

Kirsty checked her watch.

"We only have eight minutes left before we need to be back on the bus!" she said. "How are we going to get the magic sleeping bag back in time?"

"Maybe if we asked them nicely they would give it back," said Selena.

Rachel shook her head.

"They'll never agree to that," she said. "Goblins never do anything unless there's something in it for them."

"I have an idea," said Kirsty in a low voice. "Selena, could you do a spell to make the sleeping bag really uncomfortable for the goblin?"

"Oh, that's a wonderful plan!" said Rachel. "If he's not comfy in the sleeping bag, he'll get out, and we'll be able to grab it."

"I know just the spell!" said Selena with a smile.

Peeking around the corner, she waved her wand.

"Rosy posy, soft and cozy," she whispered.

A ribbon of shimmering fairy dust
coiled toward the magic sleeping bag.
The girls watched and held their breath.

Suddenly the skinny goblin started to
squirm and wriggle.

"My sleeping bag smells funny,"
he complained. "*Yuck!* It smells like
strawberries!"

"Ugh, gross!" said the goblin next to
him, holding his nose. "I can smell roses!"

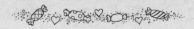

Rachel and Kirsty had to cover their mouths to keep their giggles from being heard.

"There are flower petals in here!" cried the skinny goblin. "This awful fairy sleeping bag is full of horrible fairy sweetness. Get me out of here!"

He crawled out of the sleeping bag, his nose wrinkled in disgust.

"Now's our chance!" said Rachel.

She and Kirsty ran toward the empty sleeping bag with Selena fluttering by their side.

"It's those pesky girls again!" squeaked the goblin with the orange socks. "Don't let them take the sleeping bag!"

All of the goblins leaped toward the magic sleeping bag except for the one wearing the eye mask, who stumbled in the opposite direction. The skinny goblin grabbed his arm and dragged him along, too. Before the girls could reach it, all six goblins were scrambling into the magic sleeping bag.

"Ha! You're not taking our sleeping bag!" they called out.

Selena fluttered to the ground in front of them.

"It's not your sleeping bag," she said firmly. "You shouldn't try to keep what doesn't belong to you."

"Can't hear you!" jeered the skinny goblin, sticking his fingers in his ears.

"That sleeping bag belongs to Selena!" exclaimed Rachel, her hands on her hips. "Give it back!"

The goblins zipped up the sleeping bag until all that could be seen of them was six green heads poking out at the top. They were all sticking out their tongues at the girls and making faces.

"All right," said Selena with a sly smile. "If you want to stay in the magic sleeping bag, I'll help you."

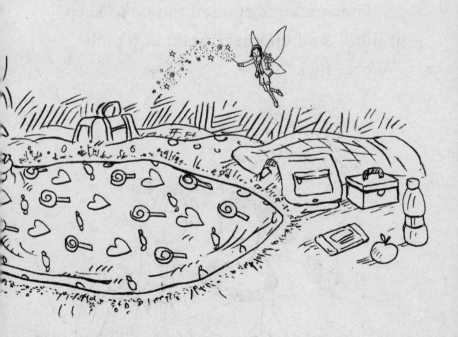

She made a sweeping, rainbow-shaped motion over the bag, then winked at Rachel and Kirsty.

"This sleeping bag is horribly soft and feathery!" complained the eye-mask goblin. "I want to get out!"

"I can't undo the zipper!" cried the goblin in checked pajamas.

"That tricky fairy used magic to keep it shut!" said another goblin in a panic. "We're stuck!"

The goblins writhed and wriggled and squawked, but they couldn't get out of the sleeping bag. Rachel and Kirsty giggled, and Selena hovered above the goblins.

"Now," she said, "are you goblins ready to make a deal?"

All Aboard!

"We'll never give you the bag!" shouted one goblin.

"Jack Frost would yell at us for a month and lock us in the dungeons!" said another.

"But I'm guessing you took the magic sleeping bag without his permission," Rachel said thoughtfully. "I bet he's already upset with you."

"How did she know that?" whispered the eye-masked goblin loudly.

"You don't like this fairy sleeping bag, do you?" asked Selena.

Six green heads shook from side to side.

"It's smelly!" said one goblin.

"It's too soft!" said another.

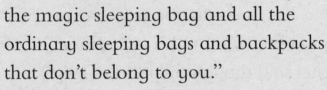

"I could use my magic to make you each a wonderful goblin sleeping bag," said Selena. "All you have to do is give back the magic sleeping bag and all the ordinary sleeping bags and backpacks that don't belong to you."

The goblins went quiet for a minute.

Their heads moved closer together as they whispered and argued.

Kirsty bit her lip anxiously. The seconds were ticking by, and it was almost time for them to be back at the bus. They couldn't leave the goblins here in the rest stop!

Then she noticed that a goblin in a pair of polka-dot pajamas was looking very red in the face. Beads of sweat were forming on his forehead.

"I'm too hot!" he moaned. "It's too squished in here. You can have the sleeping bag. Just let me out!"

"Yes, let us out!" shouted the other

goblins. "We agree! We agree!"

With a wave of her wand, Selena opened the zipper and the hot, sweet-smelling goblins tumbled out of the bag. They kicked it over to the girls.

"Now you have to keep your side of the bargain!" demanded the skinny goblin.

"Of course," said Selena with a big smile.

There were six loud popping noises, and

each goblin found a stinky green sleeping
bag under his arm. They all sniffed
eagerly.

"*Mmm*, cabbages!" said the eye-mask
goblin.

"Moldy fruit!"
squeaked another.

"Mine's all lumpy,"
said the goblin
with the orange
socks. "I think
it's full of rocks.
Yippee!"

And with that,
the goblins
rushed off in the direction of the
parking lot.

The girls turned to Selena.

"Can you use your magic to send them

back to the Ice Castle?" asked Kirsty. "I
don't like the idea of taking them to our
giant sleepover!"

"I'm sorry," said Selena. "My magic

isn't strong enough for
that. But as
soon as I've
returned the
magic sleeping bag
to its rightful home,
I'll come back to
help you at the
sleepover. After all, we still
have to find my other two magic
objects!"

Selena tapped her wand gently on
the magic sleeping bag. With a flurry
of glistening sparkles it returned to
fairy-size. Another wave of her wand

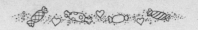

sent all the ordinary sleeping bags and backpacks back to the bus.

"I've made sure that all the goblins will sleep for the rest of the trip, so they'll stay out of trouble," she said. "Thank you both so much for helping me! I'll be back as soon as I can to help you look for the snack box and the game bag. Then all sleepovers can be fun and happy again."

"We'll do whatever we can to help," Rachel promised with a big smile.

As Selena disappeared in a swirl of shimmering fairy dust, Kirsty looked at her watch.

45

"Oh, no. We only have thirty seconds until we need to be back at the bus!" she said. "Rachel—run!"

The girls sprinted back through the rest stop, dodging the crowds of people. They ran to the bus, climbed on board, and dropped into their seats, panting and giggling.

"Cutting it close, girls," said Mr.

Ferguson, tapping his watch. He winked. "All right, we're all here now. Next stop, the National Museum!"

Rachel turned to Kirsty and grinned. Both girls were ready for the next part of their big sleepover adventure!

The Enchanted Game Bag

Contents

A Vanishing Act

The bus rolled along a wide street in
the center of the city. Kirsty and Rachel
pressed their noses up against the window.
It was almost dark, but each tree along
the pavement was lit up with sparkling
lights.

"I wonder if Selena will be waiting for
us inside the museum," said Kirsty quietly.

"We still have to find the enchanted game bag and the sleepover snack box so all sleepovers will be fun again!"

The bus pulled up in front of the National Museum. It was an amazing building! Tall pillars stood on either side of the large entrance, and the words *National Museum* were carved into the stone above the door. Mr. Ferguson stood up at the front of the bus. "We're here!" he announced. "Now remember, there are going to be a lot of different groups at the museum tonight so stay close to me."

Kirsty and Rachel eagerly filed off the

bus. The square in front of the museum
was crowded with kids, and there were
still more buses pulling up. Chatter and
laughter filled the air. Kirsty and Rachel
held each other's hand tightly and gazed
around.

There were some kids in school
uniforms and others in ordinary clothes.
The girls saw lots of Cub Scouts and Girl
Scouts, too. Ten kids were wearing green
T-shirts with NORTHBROOKS JUNIOR CHOIR
printed on them in white letters. Teachers

and group leaders were calling out
instructions, and backpacks and sleeping
bags were being hoisted onto shoulders.
It was very busy and exciting, and for a
moment the girls forgot about everything
except watching the crowd of kids.

"OK, everybody," said Mr.
Ferguson in a loud voice
that made them jump.
"Grab your things
from the luggage
area and line up
in pairs."

"Oh, Kirsty!" Rachel exclaimed. "We
have to get to the luggage area and
make sure that the goblins aren't up to
trouble!"

"But we're at the back of the line!" said
Kirsty.

The girls tried to squeeze their way to the front, but Mr. Ferguson noticed and stopped them.

"No pushing, girls," he said. "Your backpacks aren't going to walk off by themselves, don't worry."

"No," said Kirsty under her breath, "but they might walk off with goblin legs underneath them!"

"Selena cast a spell to make the goblins sleep," Rachel reminded her. "I just hope that they'll be out of sight at the 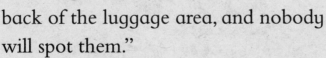 back of the luggage area, and nobody will spot them."

It seemed to take forever until the kids in front of them had collected their bags.

At last, it was their turn! Making sure
that Mr. Ferguson didn't see them, the
girls picked up their things and peered
into the shadows at the back of the
luggage area. The lights from the trees
lit up the space, and the girls could see
that, except for a few bags, the space was
empty!

"There's nothing there!" said Rachel.

"No goblins and no goblin sleeping
bags," Kirsty agreed. "But they were
supposed to be asleep!"

Rachel remembered something.

"Selena said that her spell would make the goblins sleep 'for the rest of the trip,'" she said. "They must have woken up as soon as we arrived at the museum. They probably climbed out before we got off the bus."

"Maybe they've gone back to the Ice Castle," said Kirsty hopefully.

The girls looked around at the crowds of kids heading into the museum. If the goblins were among them, they would be really tough to spot. Rachel shook her head.

"I don't think they've gone home," she said. "Keep watching out for them, Kirsty. I have a feeling that there's more goblin trouble ahead!"

The Purple Group

Kirsty and Rachel joined the back of
the line, and Mr. Ferguson led them all
into the museum. They found themselves
standing in the main entrance hall. For a
minute, all thoughts of goblins left their
minds.

The glass dome ceiling seemed to be miles above their heads, and through it they could see the moon and stars shining. The floor was covered with black and white tiles. A flight of wide stone steps curved up to the galleries, and long hallways led off to the sides. In the center of the entrance hall stood a life-size dinosaur model, its jaws gaping.

"ROOAARRR!"

Everyone squealed and giggled as the
recording echoed through the air. Then a
smiling, dark-haired lady walked toward
them, holding a clipboard.

"Good evening, kids," she said. "My
name is Charlotte. I just need to sign you
in, and then we can get the fun started."

Mr. Ferguson shook hands with
Charlotte.

"Thirty children
from Wetherbury
School," he said.

Charlotte marked
off their names on
her clipboard.

"Welcome to the
National Museum,"
she said with a
big smile. "We're

so excited to have you all here. You are
going to be in the Purple Group. You can
leave your backpacks and sleeping bags
in the storage room for now. It's over
there in the corner."

She handed Mr. Ferguson a bag of
purple hats.

"Everyone must wear one of these to
show which group they're in," she said.

"The first game will be
a gallery treasure hunt,
and each group will
be in a different gallery.
The Purple Group is
going to be in the
Roman Gallery."

"What sort of treasure are we going to
be looking for?" asked Rachel.

"Each group will follow clues to find

a letter of the alphabet," Charlotte explained. "When all the letters are put together, they'll make the name of a place in the museum. That's where the midnight feast and storytelling will be held!"

It sounded wonderful! There were lots of excited mutters and whispers among the kids. But Kirsty was worried.

"Selena's enchanted game bag is still missing," she whispered to Rachel. "Without it, the treasure hunt game

might go wrong. That would ruin the midnight feast and the storytelling, too!"

"Don't worry," said Rachel. "We won't let Jack Frost and his goblins mess things up for everyone."

The girls put their belongings in the storage room and followed Charlotte to the Roman Gallery. When they reached the gallery, Charlotte handed an envelope to each pair of kids.

"Somewhere in this gallery, a letter of the alphabet has been hidden," she said. "It's your mission to find it and bring it to the main entrance hall. The clues in these envelopes will help you. Good luck, and have fun!"

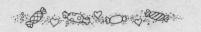

The kids rushed into the Roman
Gallery, tearing open the envelopes.
Kirsty and Rachel looked around quickly.
There were no goblins in sight.

"They're not here," said Rachel.
"Quick, Kirsty—open our clue!"

Kirsty opened the
envelope and took
out a green card.

"That's funny,"
said Rachel. "I would
have expected the
card to be purple
for the Purple Group."

The clue read:

> *Harder than glass and*
> *richer than crowns,*
> *you'll find me on fingers*
> *and fabulous gowns.*

"What does it mean?" Kirsty wondered.
"Something that's harder than glass . . .
diamonds?"

"Yes!" Rachel cried. "They're found on
fingers, too — in rings!"

"There's a diamond exhibition in the
museum," said Kirsty. "Maybe we're
supposed to look in there?"

"But Charlotte said that our clues would be about something in this gallery," Rachel replied. She frowned and paused for a minute. "Kirsty, something doesn't seem right!"

Treasure Hunt Trouble

Suddenly, a boy in a green hat came running through the door.

"Hey, I think I got one of your clues by mistake," he announced, holding up a purple card.

"Mr. Ferguson, my clue doesn't make sense," said Hannah at the same time. "It's all about sea life."

Everyone started talking at once and holding up their clues. Rachel saw red, green, blue, and yellow cards being waved in the air.

"I'm sure that our clues are supposed to be printed on purple cards," she said. "I think all the clues have been mixed up."

Kirsty and Rachel looked out through the door. They could see kids in different colored hats running between the galleries. Charlotte was standing in the middle of them all, frantically checking her clipboard.

"This is all because the enchanted game bag is missing," said Rachel in a low voice. "Oh, Kirsty. The treasure hunt is going to be ruined! I wish there was something we could do."

"Maybe there is," said Kirsty, her eyes shining.

She pointed at the display behind Rachel. One of the ancient Roman vases was glowing! Suddenly, Selena zoomed out of it and waved at the girls through the glass display cabinet. Then, with a tiny flash of fairy dust, she appeared outside of the cabinet.

The girls crouched down behind the display as Selena fluttered over and perched on Kirsty's knee.

"I have good news!" she said, her cheeks pink with excitement. "I've seen the enchanted game bag! A boy wearing a red hat has it in his bag."

Kirsty gasped. "How did he get it?"

"One of the goblins must have dropped it," said Rachel thoughtfully. "I bet the boy saw it and picked it up."

"Let's go and find him now," Selena pleaded.

Rachel and Kirsty nodded, but before they could move they saw a very short

kid rushing past the door of the Roman Gallery. He was wearing a green hat pulled low over his face, but that didn't fool the girls for a minute.

"That was a goblin!" cried Kirsty.

"Oh, no. I hope they didn't get the enchanted game bag back!" said Selena.

"Quick, let's follow him," said Rachel.

"It'll be easier if you're fairy-size, like me," Selena declared.

The girls ducked into an alcove where they couldn't be seen. Selena waved her wand, and for a moment a shimmering star of fairy dust hung in the air in front of the girls. Then it dissolved into hundreds of miniature stars that enveloped Rachel and Kirsty in a magic glow. They closed

their eyes and felt themselves shrinking to fairy-size, their toes and fingertips tingling. When they opened their eyes, they were hovering in the air beside Selena, fluttering their delicate wings.

"Come on," said Rachel. "We have to catch that goblin!"

They flew out of the Roman Gallery and spotted the goblin running down the stone staircase. All the groups were upstairs and the museum was closed, so the main entrance hall should have been empty. But when the girls reached the bottom of the staircase, they saw that the big reception desk was fully staffed — by five goblins!

One goblin was tearing entrance tickets off a long strip, and another was wearing headphones and listening to a museum

tour. A third was pressing all the buttons on the cash register and making them beep. The skinniest goblin was sitting on a revolving chair while another goblin spun him around and around, giggling.

Selena and the girls hid behind the dinosaur model as the goblin in the green hat rushed up to the desk.

"I can't find the pesky kid who picked up the fairy bag," he wailed. "They all look the same to me."

"We'll all have to go and look," said the skinny goblin. "Come on!"

Rachel looked at Kirsty and Selena in alarm. "We have to find that boy before the goblins do!" she said in an urgent whisper.

78

Kirsty and Selena nodded, determined. Together, the three fairies immediately flitted back up to the galleries, and zoomed off in three different directions. This was a race against time!

Finders Keepers

Rachel darted down a long hallway, peering closely at any boy she saw wearing a red hat. But none of them was carrying anything that looked like a magic object. Then she noticed a boy sitting alone on a bench in the Dinosaur

Gallery. He was wearing a Boy Scout
uniform and a red hat. Unlike most of
the other kids, he still had his bag with
him. He unzipped it and pulled out a
bottle of water.

As he was drinking, Rachel saw that
there was a faint glow coming from the
bag. This had to be the boy who had
picked up Selena's enchanted game bag!
She fluttered off to look for Kirsty and
Selena.

They were both hovering at the top of
the stairs, having searched everywhere
else.

"I found him!" Rachel said in
excitement. "Follow me!"

When Rachel, Kirsty, and Selena
flew into the Dinosaur Gallery, they
were shocked. A goblin was creeping

82

up behind the boy — and his little green
hand was just about to grab the boy's
bag!

At the last moment, the boy stood up
and picked up his bag. The goblin's hand
closed on empty air, and the girls all
heaved sighs of relief.

"That was close," said Kirsty.

"The goblins don't give up that easily,"
said Rachel. "Look!"

The boy had stopped beside a model
of a green-skinned dinosaur. His bag was
on his back, but he hadn't zipped it up
properly. And hanging off the back of the
dinosaur was the goblin in the green hat!

This time, the goblin actually got his
hand into the bag. Then the boy seemed
to sense that something was wrong. He

turned sharply, but the goblin had slid
back behind the dinosaur.

Looking confused, the boy walked
out of the Dinosaur Gallery. He headed
through a small room to the Arctic
Display. The goblins scurried after him,
and the girls fluttered above.

"How are we going to get the
enchanted game bag back now?" asked
Selena.

The girls could hear the worry in her
voice. They put their arms around her
shoulder.

"Don't worry, Selena," said Kirsty. "If
you turn us back into humans, we'll talk
to the boy."

"We'll get the bag back for you,"
Rachel promised.

They fluttered to the ground as the boy

wandered around the display, reading the descriptions of life in the Arctic Ocean. He paused beside a model of a polar bear and stroked its fur. The two goblins scrambled up the back of the polar bear and teetered on its head. One of them held the other by the ankles and dangled him down toward the bag. "Oh, no — look!" cried Kirsty. "Selena, hurry!"

Selena swept her wand over their heads. In a flash of fairy dust, they were human-size again. They leaped out in front of the boy as Selena tucked herself under Kirsty's hair.

"Look out!" Rachel shouted.

The boy spun around, and the goblin on top of the polar bear lost his balance. He let go of the goblin in the green hat, who landed on the ground with a loud squawk of fury. The first goblin looked scared, and ran out of the room before he could be yelled at.

"Are you trying to steal from me?" the boy demanded. "Leave me alone!"

"Give me that game bag NOW!" the goblin cried rudely.

The boy looked really angry.

"I don't like people who try to steal from me," he said. "I found that bag. Finders keepers!"

Rachel and Kirsty exchanged alarmed looks. What if the boy refused to give the enchanted game bag back to them, too? They needed a plan — and fast! But what?

A Lesson in Manners

"Excuse me," said Rachel.

The boy turned to look at her. "Oh, hello," he said. "Thank you for warning me!"

"You're welcome," Rachel replied. "We've actually been looking for you, too. I think you have something that belongs to a friend of ours."

Kirsty stepped forward with a friendly
smile. "Our friend lost her game bag," she
explained. "Without it, lots of kids will be
really disappointed, because their games
won't work properly."

"She really needs it back," Rachel
added "Can you please help us?"

The boy peered at them thoughtfully,
then looked at the green-hatted goblin,
who was pouting angrily.

"This boy has been trying to take the
bag from me," he said. "It must be very
special."

"It is," said Kirsty. "It was stolen from
our friend, too."

The boy reached into his own bag and
pulled out the game bag. He looked at it
thoughtfully for a minute. Then he smiled
and held it out to Rachel.

"It sounds like your friend needs this
more than I do," he said.

"Thank you so much!" said Rachel and
Kirsty together.

With a snort of rage, the goblin ran
past the girls and out of the room. The
boy raised his eyebrows.

"Maybe that'll teach him a lesson about manners," he said. "I'd better go and find my group now. Good-bye!"

"Bye!" called the girls as he hurried out.

After he'd gone, Selena flitted out and hovered in front of Rachel and Kirsty. With a flick of her wand, the enchanted game bag returned to fairy-size. Selena smiled at the girls.

"Thank you for persuading him to give back the bag!" she said. "You did a wonderful job."

"You're welcome," said Rachel. "Are you going to take the bag back to Fairyland now?"

"Yes," Selena replied. "That will fix the treasure hunt problems. But I'll come right back—we still have to find the sleepover snack box so the midnight feast will be a success."

With that, she smiled and disappeared in a flurry of fairy dust.

"Come on," said Kirsty, grabbing Rachel's hand. "Let's get back to the Roman Gallery."

They walked back to their group.

When they arrived, Mr. Ferguson was looking very happy.

"Good news, girls!" he said. "Charlotte has just found some brand-new sets of clues, and our team has already figured out the puzzles. Our letter is *C*. I'm sorry you missed the chance to solve the clues."

"We don't mind at all," said Rachel, sharing a secret smile with Kirsty.

Now that everything was back to normal, it didn't take long for all the

groups to complete their treasure hunts.
All together, they found five letters. There
was a purple *C*, a green *Y*, a blue *T*, a
yellow *P*, and a red *R*. Everyone gathered
in the entrance hall, and Charlotte held
up her hand for silence.

"When you put these letters in the right
order, they will spell out the place where
we're having the midnight feast and

storytelling," she said. "Who will be the first to figure it out?"

A hand shot into the air. It was the Boy Scout in the red hat—the boy who had found the enchanted game bag.

"It spells 'crypt,'" he said.

"Correct," said Charlotte, sounding impressed. "The midnight feast is being

held in the old crypt, deep underneath
the museum."

Rachel and Kirsty looked at each other,
thrilled. A midnight feast in a crypt? How
exciting!

The Sleepover
Snack Box

Contents

Into the Crypt!

"I can feel butterflies in my stomach, I'm so excited!" whispered Kirsty in Rachel's ear.

Charlotte, the organizer of the museum's giant sleepover, asked everyone to line up in pairs. She handed each of them a little lantern with four glass sides and a curved handle.

"We're about to go down to the crypt, where the midnight feast is being held," she said. "It's dark down there and a little bit spooky, so hold on to your lanterns!"

There were lots of gasps and giggles, and Rachel and Kirsty both felt thrilled. They were near the front of the line, and they followed Charlotte down a winding stone staircase to the depths of the museum.

It grew colder and darker as they traveled deeper underground. At last,

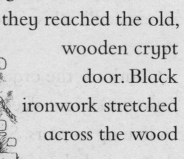 they reached the old, wooden crypt door. Black ironwork stretched across the wood

in the shapes of coiling branches and vines. Charlotte pushed the door open, and it gave a loud *CREEEAAAK!*

"Oooh!" said Hannah, who was standing in front of Rachel.

Charlotte led the way into the dark crypt. A narrow passageway lay in front of them, and the lanterns made shadows flicker across the stone walls.

"This is where we keep all the exhibits

that aren't being used," Charlotte said.
"The crypt is very, very big, with lots
of tunnels leading off of it. We haven't
mapped all of them yet, so I don't want
anyone going off exploring!"

Rachel and Kirsty saw dark archways
on either side of them.

"Where do they lead to?" asked Kirsty.

"Some of the tunnels go right under the
city," Charlotte replied.

Her voice echoed around them,

bouncing off the stone walls. Rachel
thought about the long, dark tunnels
stretching underneath the city's houses
and shops. They sounded so mysterious
and exciting!

The light from their lanterns made a
glowing circle around the group as they
walked. The girls saw shadowy boxes
and tall, decorative vases standing on the
floor. There were lots of strange shapes
covered in white sheets.

The long line of kids wound through the crypt, passing tall shelves crammed with dusty crates. At last, the passageway widened out into a room. In the center of the room, a man was sitting on a fancy wooden chair with purple cushions. There was a map on the table in front of him.

"Gather 'round, everyone!" said Charlotte. "This is Zack the storyteller. He will be entertaining you after your midnight feast!"

The storyteller smiled at them. Rachel

and Kirsty thought he looked nice. He had twinkling brown eyes that shone in the lamplight, and a long, nut-brown beard.

On the far side of the crypt was a red velvet curtain, which stretched across the whole width of the room. While the kids gathered in a group, Charlotte walked over to the curtain and peeked behind it.

The girls caught a glimpse of a long wooden table before Charlotte let the curtain fall back. When she

turned around, she was frowning.

"Charlotte looks worried," Kirsty whispered. "I wonder what's wrong."

Charlotte hurried over to Zack the storyteller. The girls edged a little closer.

"There's a bit of a problem," they heard Charlotte say. "The picnic food for the

feast isn't on the table. Could you start your story early while I go to check what's happened?"

Kirsty and Rachel exchanged alarmed looks.

"Oh, no!" said Rachel. "This must be because the magic sleepover snack box is still missing!"

Selena Appears

"Could everyone sit in a semicircle around the storyteller, please?" asked Charlotte. "There has been a slight change of plan. The story will start now, before the midnight feast. But don't worry—soon it will be time to eat!"

Her voice sounded reassuring and confident, but Rachel and Kirsty could see worry in her eyes. The other kids took their places around the storyteller, but the girls remained standing as they watched Charlotte leave. They couldn't help worrying about Selena's sleepover snack box. While it was missing, things would keep going wrong with sleepover snacks everywhere!

"Sit down, girls," said Mr. Ferguson.

 Rachel and Kirsty looked around and realized that everyone was waiting for them! They took the only spots left, which were right at the back of the crowd.

They put their lanterns down, and
all the glimmering lights made a large
glowing circle around them.

"Welcome to the crypt," said Zack in
a rich, warm voice. "This place is full of
secrets, and many exciting things have
happened here. But most mysterious of all
was the puzzle of the museum ghost. . . ."

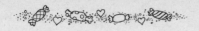

Rachel started listening to the story, but Kirsty was distracted. She kept thinking that someone was behind her. When she turned her head to look over her shoulder, she glimpsed a spiky-headed shadow!

"Rachel!" she said in an urgent whisper. "Look!"

Rachel looked around, but the strange shadow had completely disappeared.

"What was it?" she asked.

"It was a weird shadow," said Kirsty. "It looked like Jack Frost! But I must be imagining things."

"Maybe it was the lights from the lanterns making funny shapes on the wall?" Rachel suggested hopefully.

She looked down at their lanterns and gave a little gasp of surprise. The light in her lantern was fizzing and sputtering. It grew brighter and brighter. Then the little glass door shot open—and Selena zoomed out! She fluttered inside Kirsty's jacket so she wouldn't be seen by any of the other kids.

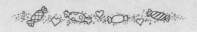

"I have news!" she whispered. "Jack Frost is fed up with the goblins losing things. He has taken  the sleepover snack box himself, and he's determined to hang on to it!"

"Oh, Selena! I think he's here!" whispered Kirsty. "I'm pretty sure I just saw his shadow."

Selena nodded, looking worried. "He's searching for the goblins so he can punish them for losing the magic sleeping bag and the enchanted game bag," she said. "I bet he knows they're here, and they're hiding from him."

The girls looked around. Zack was well into his story now, and everyone's

attention was on him.

"Nobody will notice if we slip away," said Rachel in a low voice. "Selena, can you turn us into fairies? Then we can fly around the crypt and find out what Jack Frost is up to."

"And we can try to get the sleepover snack box back, too," added Kirsty. "Jack Frost is sure to have it with him!"

"Bring your lanterns," said Selena. "They'll help us search."

The girls crept after Selena into a corner of the crypt. Once they were well-hidden, the fairy waved her tiny wand. There was a faint sound like a far-off lullaby,

and the girls shrank to the size of fairies with wings fluttering on their backs. Even their lanterns had shrunk to fairy-size!

"We must look like tiny fireflies!" Rachel giggled as they rose up into the air.

The three fairies fluttered around the edges of the room where the other kids and Zack were sitting, careful to stay out of sight.

"I'm glad it's so dark in here," said Kirsty. "Hopefully no one will notice that we're missing."

"Everyone is listening to Zack," said Rachel. "We just have to make sure we're back before the story ends!"

Things That Go Bump in the Night

There was a wide tunnel entrance close by.

"Let's start by looking down there," suggested Kirsty.

Flying as close together as they could, the three friends headed slowly down the dark tunnel.

Their tiny lanterns made pinprick
lights against the arched brick overhead.
Suddenly, they saw some bulky shapes on
the ground below them.

"What are those?" asked Selena.

"They're big packing crates," said
Rachel. "I remember Mom and Dad

using the same
sort of boxes
when we
moved to
our new
house. The
museum
must
have stored
some old
exhibits in them."

They all flew lower and saw that the

packing crates were stacked in high piles. But before they could get too close, they heard a bang and a loud squawk.

"What was that?" cried Kirsty in alarm.

"It sounded like a goblin," said Selena. "Come on!"

They flew even lower, and as their eyes adjusted to the light, they saw a goblin sitting on the ground and rubbing his foot.

"What's the matter with you?" snapped another goblin, coming out of the shadows. "Do you want Jack Frost to hear you?"

"I banged my foot!" wailed the first goblin.

Just then, there was a crash and a muffled yell from a pile of boxes against the tunnel wall. A third goblin crawled out from among the boxes, rubbing a big red bump on his head.

"A dumb box just fell on me!" he grumbled. "I don't like it down here! You

said there was going to be a midnight
feast, but it's cold and dark, and I'm
hungry."

"You'll feel even worse if Jack Frost
catches us!" hissed the first goblin. "Be
quiet!"

"You can't tell us what to do!"
squawked the goblin who had bumped
his head.

He flung himself on the first goblin and
knocked him down. The
other goblin
jumped on top
of them both,
yelling.

Selena
looked at the
girls. "If Jack
Frost were down

here, he'd have come running by now,"
she said. "Come on, let's look somewhere
else."

They flew back along the tunnel and
out into the main room. As they were
fluttering toward the next tunnel, Rachel
gave a little cry and quickly put her
hand over her mouth.

"I see Jack Frost!" she whispered to Selena and Kirsty.

Sure enough, Jack Frost was skulking around in the shadows behind the group of kids. He was edging closer and closer to them . . . and the sleepover snack box was tucked under his arm!

Selena, Rachel, and Kirsty zoomed out of sight behind a statue.

"We have to get Jack Frost away from the other kids," said Kirsty. "It's a little spooky down here anyway, and Zack is telling them a ghost story. If they see Jack Frost they'll be really scared."

They fluttered onto the head of another statue and peered around the points of its crown. Jack Frost still stood in the shadows, not moving.

"Why is he just standing there?" asked Selena.

"I think he wants to hear the story,"

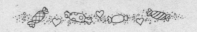

said Rachel suddenly. "He's forgotten all
about looking for the goblins!"

That gave Kirsty an idea. "Maybe
we should try to remind him about the
goblins," she suggested. "That might make
him leave the group."

"But how can we do that?" asked
Selena.

"Do you think you could use your magic to make our voices sound like goblins?" asked Kirsty. "If he heard us talking, maybe he'd follow us."

"Kirsty, that's a great idea!" said Rachel.

"You'll have to make sure he doesn't catch you," said Selena, looking

concerned. "It could be dangerous." She peeked out at Jack Frost again.

"Don't worry," said Rachel with a grin. "I'm sure we can move faster than Jack Frost!"

Midnight Mayhem

Selena waved her wand toward Rachel and Kirsty, and whispered a magic spell.

"Squawks and wails and nasty jeers;
Sounds that grate upon the ears.
Hide their sweet and girly tones
And let Jack Frost hear goblin moans."

Rachel and Kirsty both coughed, then stared at each other.

"Did it work?" asked Kirsty in a gruff goblin voice.

"Yes!" Rachel said with a squeaky goblin giggle. "Come on, let's lead Jack Frost away from the other kids!"

Rachel and Kirsty swooped down and perched on a shelf behind Jack Frost. Selena hovered above them to watch what happened.

"He'll never find us!" whispered Kirsty in a goblin-like sneer.

"Silly Jack Frost!" said Rachel, giggling.

Jack Frost's head whipped around, and the girls pressed themselves up against the wall. His eyes darted back and forth, but

of course he couldn't see any goblins.

As soon as he turned back to face Zack, Rachel and Kirsty flew a little farther away from him and hid in the folds of a sheet.

"Let's hide down here," said Kirsty in her goblin voice.

"I don't like it here—I'm going back up to the museum," added Rachel, sounding exactly like a glum goblin.

Jack Frost turned around again, scowling. He stomped toward them.

"I'm going to teach those goblins a lesson they won't forget!" the girls heard him mutter.

Rachel, Kirsty, and Selena zipped into the entrance of a nearby tunnel. They paused next to a statue draped in a sheet.

"Jack Frost's too much of a scaredy-cat to look for us down here," said Rachel loudly, snickering like a goblin.

Jack Frost bared his teeth when he heard that! He took a few steps into the tunnel.

"It's working!" whispered Selena, hovering beside Rachel and Kirsty. "Say something else!"

But just then, Zack reached a very spooky part of his story and raised his voice. Jack Frost paused and turned to listen.

"The ghost floated toward the unsuspecting children, and . . ." Zack said.

Jack Frost was enthralled. Rachel and

Kirsty whispered and giggled like goblins, but he didn't seem to hear them. He was too interested in the story!

"Oh, no!" whispered Rachel. "What are we going to do now?"

They fluttered closer to Jack Frost, who was still rooted to the spot. The sleepover snack box was tucked tightly under his arm.

"We'll just have to try reasoning with

him," said Selena. She lifted her hands helplessly.

As she did, the light from Rachel's lantern cast her shadow onto the wall next to Jack Frost. But because the wall was curved, it made her shadow giant-sized!

As he listened to the scary ghost story, Jack Frost suddenly saw a shadowy monster looming over him, its arms raised high above his head. He gave a choked cry of terror, clutched his spiky head with both hands, and ran away!

"He dropped the box!" exclaimed
Rachel, darting down to it.

Kirsty and Selena were close behind
her. Selena transformed the box to its
Fairyland size with a touch of her wand.
Then she waved her wand toward the
girls again.

"It's nice to have my own voice back!"
Kirsty laughed, rubbing her throat.

"Yes, I'm happy not to sound like a
goblin anymore," said Rachel.

But before they could say anything
else, the sheet on the statue next to them
moved. The girls held their breath and
clasped hands as a green goblin face
appeared.

Scary Shadows

Selena and the girls pressed themselves back against the tunnel wall. The goblin hadn't spotted them!

"He's gone!" hissed the goblin. "Now's our chance!"

The sheet slipped to the ground, and

the girls gasped. Instead of a statue, they
saw six goblins standing on one another's
shoulders. They looked awfully wobbly!

"I've had enough of sleepovers!"
wheezed the goblin at the bottom. "Let's
get out of here!"

They jumped down and darted out of the tunnel. The girls heaved sighs of relief.

"Thank goodness!" said Rachel. "Jack Frost and the goblins are gone, and we found the sleepover snack box. Everything is back to normal."

"You've both been wonderful!" said Selena, hugging them tightly. "I'm so happy to have all my magic objects back where they belong!"

"And we're happy to have helped," said Kirsty, hugging her back.

"I have to take the sleepover snack

box to Fairyland," said Selena. "But I'll never forget what you've done for me today— and for sleepovers all over the world!" She waved her wand, and in a flash of fairy dust the girls had returned to their normal size.

"Good-bye," said Selena with a beaming smile. "I hope I'll see you again one day!"

"We hope so, too!" said the girls together. "Good-bye!"

The air filled with shimmering golden fairy dust. When it cleared, Selena had disappeared. Rachel and Kirsty smiled at each other happily, and then the sound of applause filled the air.

"That must mean that the story is over!" Kirsty gasped. "Quick!"

They raced out of the tunnel and slipped back into their places—just as

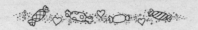

Mr. Ferguson turned to look at them!

"Did you enjoy the story, girls?" he asked.

"It was a very exciting adventure!" said Rachel with a grin.

Just then, Charlotte appeared with two delivery men. They were carrying huge catering trays filled with delicious-smelling food.

"The delivery van was caught in a traffic jam," Charlotte explained to Mr. Ferguson. "But the food's here now!"

She whisked the curtain aside and revealed a long table. The delivery men laid out dishes filled with sandwiches, salads, and sausage rolls. There were bowls of chips, cups of Jell-O, individual

ice creams, platters of iced cupcakes, and lots of strawberries and blueberries.

"Time for the feast!" Charlotte announced.

All of the kids rushed to the table in

excitement. Rachel and Kirsty chatted quietly about their adventures as they snacked on the delicious food. In an amazingly short time, every single bit had been eaten.

"Now it really is time for bed . . ." said
Charlotte.

There were groans from everyone, and
her eyes twinkled.

". . . after a game of hide-and-seek, of
course!" she said with a laugh.

There was a loud cheer, and the kids
picked up their lanterns and got into
pairs again.

"This has been one of our most exciting adventures yet," said Kirsty as they headed back up to the museum. "So much has happened today!"

"I'm really glad that we found all of Selena's magic objects in time," Rachel added. "Now we can relax and enjoy the sleepover."

"And the game of hide-and-seek," said Kirsty with a happy smile. "It's the perfect end to a truly magical adventure!"

SPECIAL EDITION

There's another fairy adventure
just around the corner!
Join Rachel
and Kirsty as they help

Cara
the Camp Fairy!

Read on for a special sneak peek. . . .

Goblin Tracks

"I can't believe we're actually at summer camp together!" Rachel Walker said happily.

"Me, neither," said her best friend, Kirsty Tate. "We get to do some of our favorite things all in one place. And we get to do them together!"

Rachel and Kirsty had met on vacation on beautiful Rainspell Island. Since they lived in different towns, they didn't get to see each other every day. So when the girls' parents had suggested they go to Camp Oakwood, both Rachel and Kirsty were excited.

Now, on their second day of camp, the two girls sat at a table in the Craft Cabin. They were making pictures with yarn.

"First, sketch your picture on the paper," explained Bollie, their camp counselor. Bollie's real name was Margaret Bolleran, but everyone called her Bollie.

Rachel sketched a fairy on her paper. She looked over at Kirsty and saw that she had sketched a fairy, too.

The girls smiled at each other.

"Now spread the glue over the places you would normally color in," Bollie said. "Then you can curl up pieces of yarn and place them on the glue, like this."

She held up a picture of a tree with green yarn for leaves and brown yarn on the trunk . . . but then the yarn slid off and plopped on one of Bollie's boots.

"That's weird," she said, feeling the paper. "This glue isn't sticky at all."

"My glue isn't sticking, either," complained a red-haired girl.

Bollie frowned. "Maybe it's too hot," she said, pushing her blonde bangs out of her eyes. "I know! Let's have some fun with the paint spinner, instead."

Bollie walked to a big machine on a

table on the side of the room. Rachel,
Kirsty, and the other girls gathered
around to watch.

"It's easy," Bollie said, her green eyes
shining. "You put paper on the bottom.
Then you turn on the spinner and
squeeze in drops of paint."

She held a plastic bottle of orange
paint over the spinner and squeezed it.
With a *pop*, the cover slipped off! Instead
of a few drops, the whole bottle of paint
gushed into the spinner.

"Everybody duck!" Bollie yelled.

Rachel and Kirsty ducked down as
quickly as they could. Orange paint
splattered everywhere! Bollie turned
off the machine, but not before every
camper was covered in orange dots.

"Oh, no!" some of the girls wailed.

Rachel giggled. "It's like we're covered in sprinkles," she said.

But Bollie did not look happy. "Everybody head to the sinks to clean up!" she told them. "Craft time is canceled. We're going on a hike!"

The campers quickly washed off the paint and changed into clean green-and-white Camp Oakwood tank tops. They lined up at the edge of the woods.

"Follow me, and stick to the path," Bollie advised them.

Rachel and Kirsty hung back at the end of the line.

"Rachel, why do you think that happened in the Craft Cabin?" Kirsty asked in a whisper.

Rachel gave her a meaningful look. "It feels like Jack Frost to me."

"But what would Jack Frost be doing at summer camp?" Kirsty wondered. "He likes to be in the cold, doesn't he?"

Just then, Bollie stopped suddenly on the path. "Look! Here are some tracks we can examine," she said.

The campers made a circle around Bollie as she bent down to give the tracks a closer look.

"That's strange," she said. "I thought maybe they'd be deer prints or raccoon tracks. But these look like big, bare feet. Who would walk around the woods in bare feet?"

Rachel and Kirsty knew exactly who would do that.

Goblins!

RAINBOW magic

These activities are magical!
Play dress-up, send friendship notes, and much more!

SCHOLASTIC
www.scholastic.com
www.rainbowmagiconline.com

HIT entertainment

RMACTIV3